The Queen Bee

Cataloguing in Publication Data

[Bienenkonigin. English]
The queen bee / Brothers Grimm; Elizabeth James, translator;
Iassen Ghiuselev, illustrator.

ISBN 0-9688768-4-6

1. Fairy tales—Germany. I. Grimm, Jacob, 1785-1863. II. Grimm, Wilhelm, 1786-1859.
III. Ghiuselev, Iassen, 1964- IV. James, Elizabeth, 1958- V, Title.
PZ8.B45 2003   j398.2'0943   C2002-911370-9

Published in 2003 by Simply Read Books Inc.

Designed by Steedman Design, Vancouver, Canada
Typeset in Mrs. Eaves

Printed and bound in Belgium

Simply Read Books Inc.
501-5525 West Boulevard
Vancouver, B.C. V6M 3W6
www.simplyreadbooks.com

The Queen Bee

Written by the Brothers Grimm
Translated by Elizabeth James

Illustrated by Iassen Ghiuselev

Simply Read Books

Once there were two princes who went in search of adventure. They began to lead a wild, reckless way of life and resigned never to return home again. Their youngest brother, who was called Dimwit, decided to go and find them. When he found them at last, they ridiculed him for wanting to make his own way in the world while they, who were considered smarter, had managed to achieve nothing.

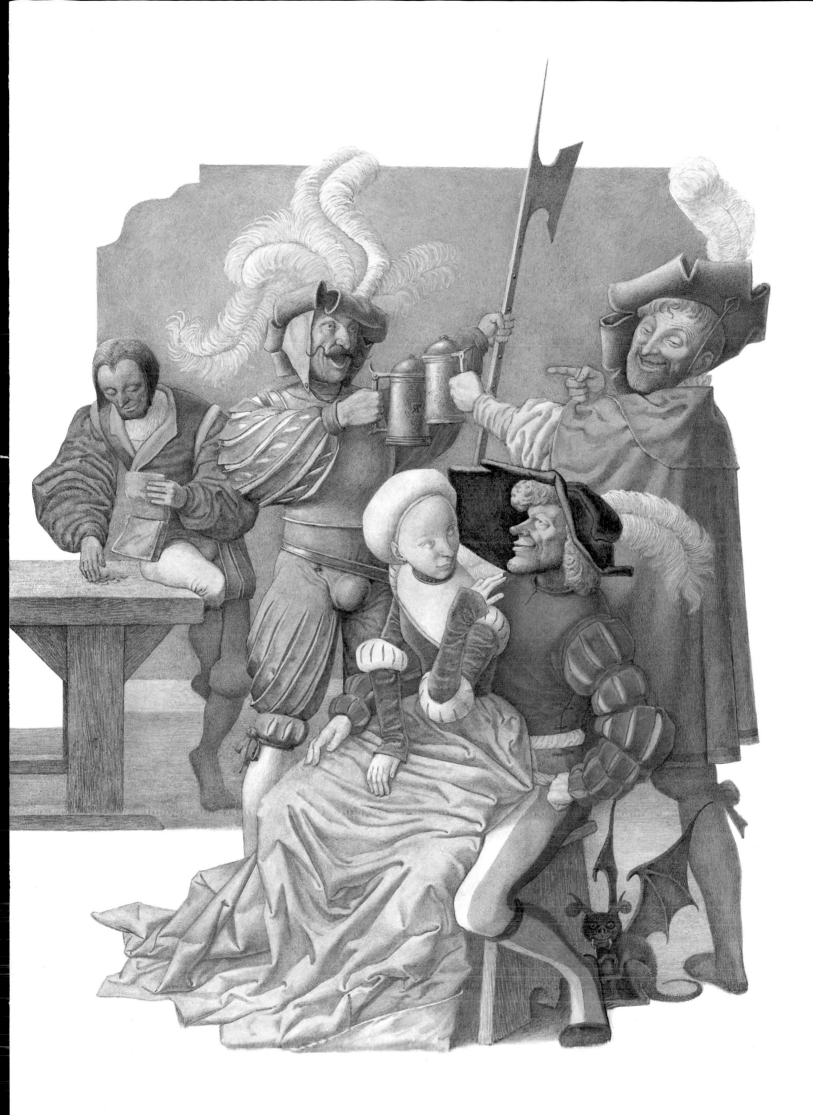

All three set out together and came to an anthill along the way. The eldest brothers wanted to stir it up and watch the frightened little ants carry away their eggs but Dimwit said, "Leave the ants in peace. I don't want you to disturb them."

They went on further and came to a flock of ducks at a lake. The two eldest brothers wanted to catch a few and roast them, but Dimwit would not let them and said, "Leave the ducks in peace. I don't want you to kill them."

Eventually they came to a nest of bees in a tree. The honey was over-flowing and ran down the trunk. The two eldest brothers wanted to light a fire under the tree to suffocate the bees and collect the honey, but Dimwit stopped them again and said, "Leave the bees in peace. I don't want you to burn them."

The three brothers finally came to a castle and witnessed horses made of stone in the stables. They inspected all the rooms and did not find a single soul anywhere, until they came to a door with three locks. Through a small opening in the door, they saw a little gray man sitting at a table.

He did not hear them when they called to him the first and second time, but the third time he got up, unlocked the door and came out. Without speaking a word, he led them to a banquet table. After they were finished eating and drinking, he showed each of them to a room for the night.

The next morning, the little gray man went to the eldest brother and signaled him to follow. He led him to a stone monument. On it were inscribed three tasks to be fulfilled in order to undo the spell that was cast on the castle.

The first task was to find a thousand crystals belonging to the king's daughter that were hidden beneath the moss in the forest. Whoever missed a single crystal by sunset would be turned to stone. The eldest brother searched all day for the crystals. By sunset he had only found one hundred and was turned to stone. The next day, the second brother took over the task. At the end of the day, he had found only two hundred crystals and was also turned to stone.

Finally it was Dimwit's turn to search for the crystals. It was a very slow and difficult task. As he sat down on a stone and began to cry, along came the ant king with five thousand ants he had saved. In a short time, the tiny insects collected every crystal and put them together in a pile.

The second task was to get the key to the princess's bedroom from the bottom of the lake. When Dimwit got to the lake, along swam the ducks he had saved. They dived under the lake and brought back the key from the depths.

The third task was the hardest of all. Dimwit had to choose which sleeping princess was the King's youngest and dearest. They looked exactly alike, except that each one had eaten something different before falling asleep. The oldest had eaten a piece of sugar, the second some syrup, and the youngest a spoonful of honey. Just then, along came the queen bee that Dimwit had saved from burning. The queen bee tasted the lips of all three and paused on the princess who had eaten the honey. The prince then knew the right one to choose.

At last the spell was broken, and the castle and all its residents came
back to life. Dimwit married the king's youngest and dearest daughter
and became the king after her father died. His two brothers married
the other two sisters.